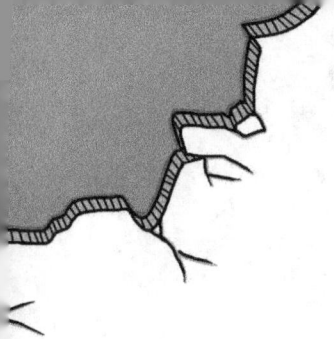

Copyright © 2014, Richard Smith World Rights Reserved

Published by Crystal Sea Studios
crystalsea.rsmith@gmail.com

www.facebook.com/maskgraphicnovel
https://twitter.com/@CrystalSeaComic

Third Edition 2014
ISBN: 978-0-9924664-1-1

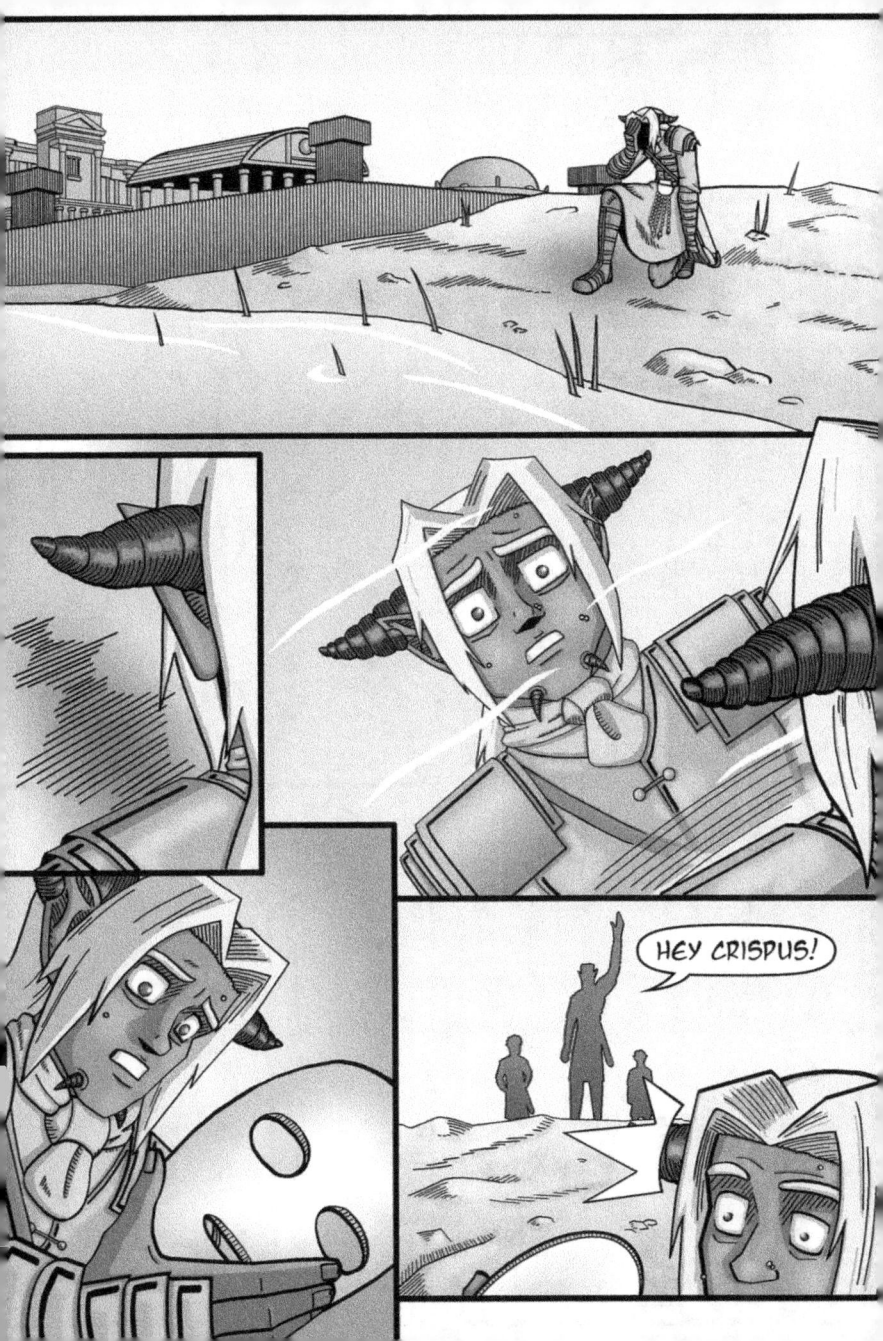

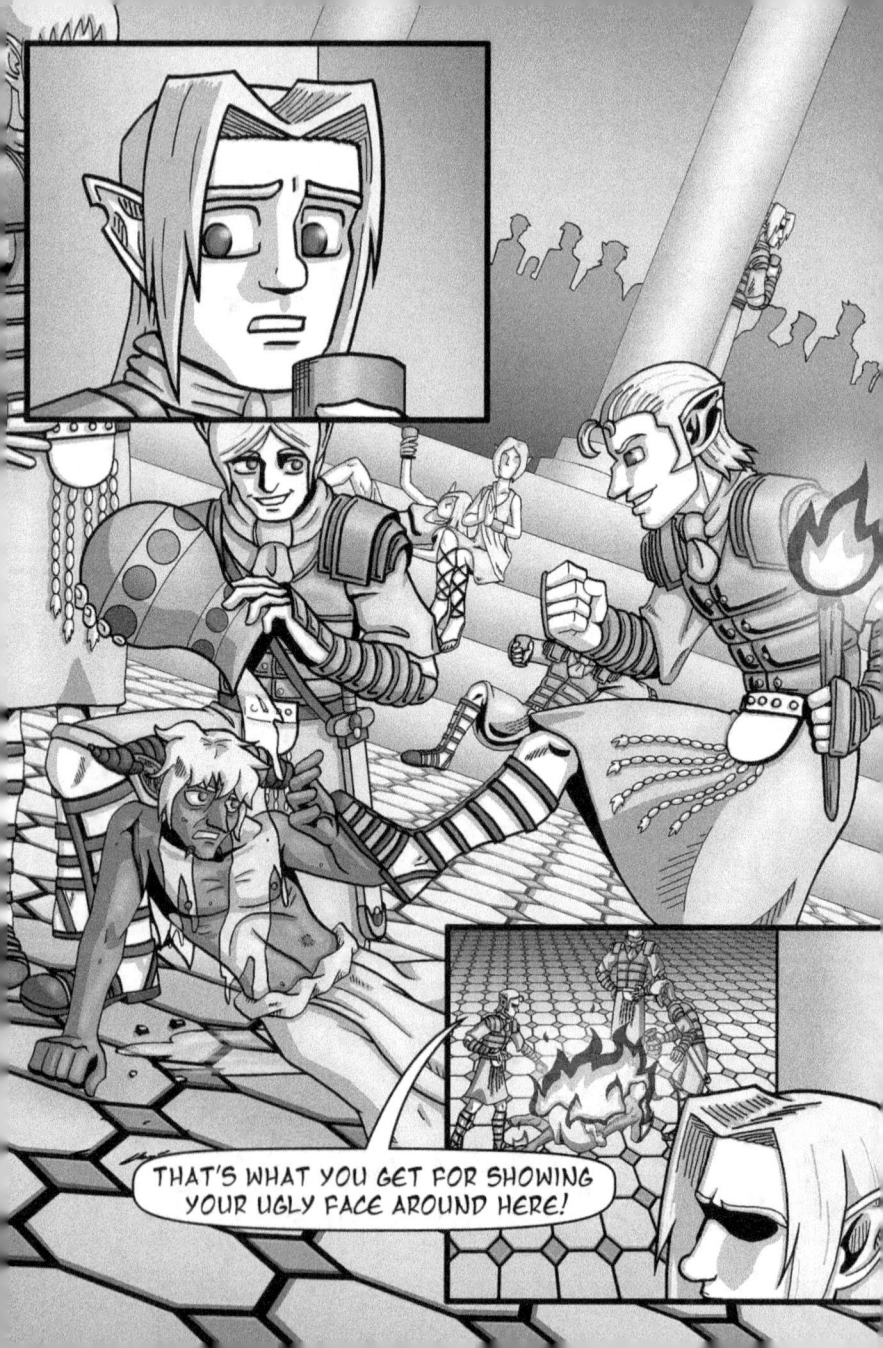

WHAT'RE YOU DOING HERE, YOU WALLFLOWER?

AVE THERE!

YOU REMEMBER LUCESTIA.

UM, AVE.

WANNA HANG OUT?

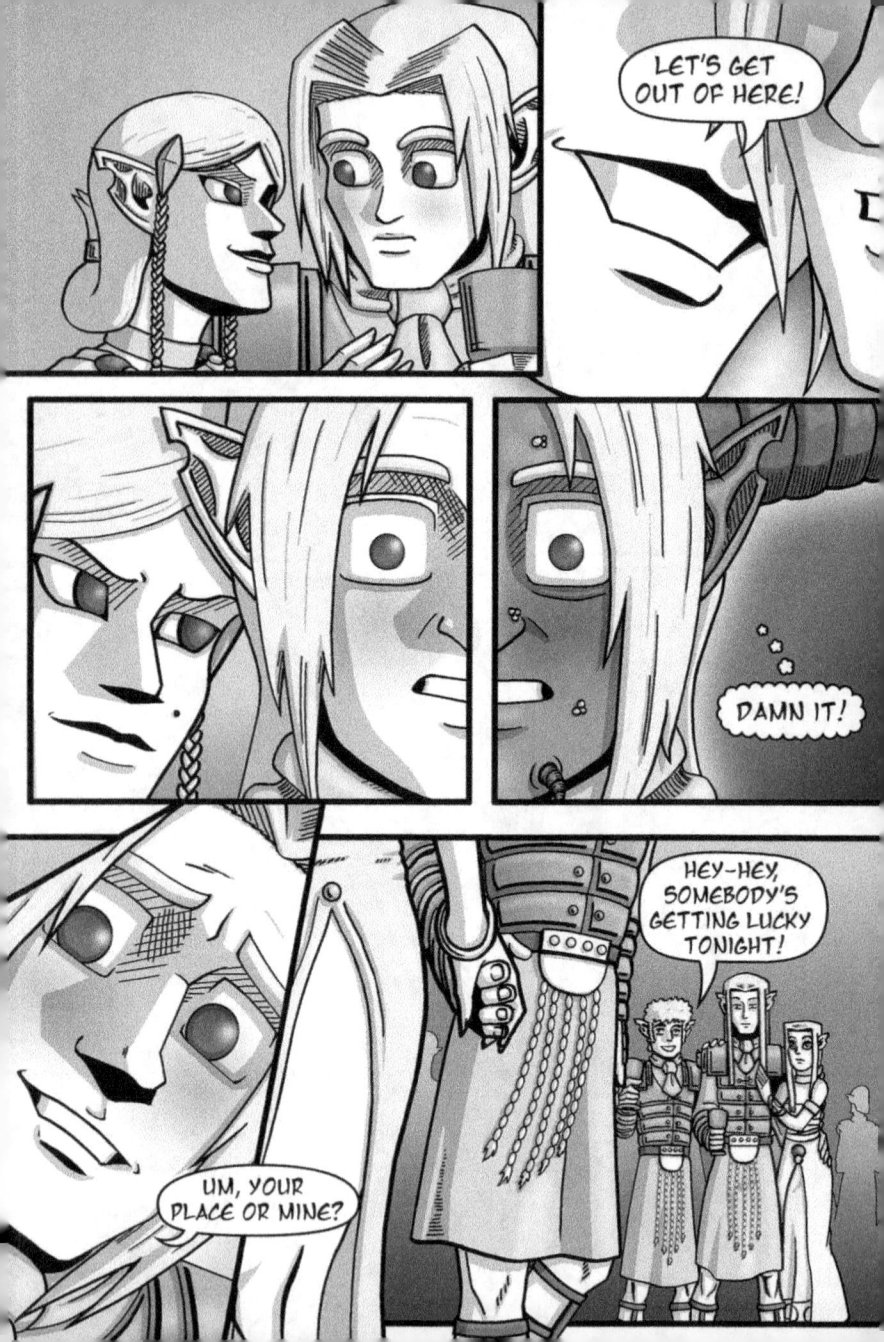

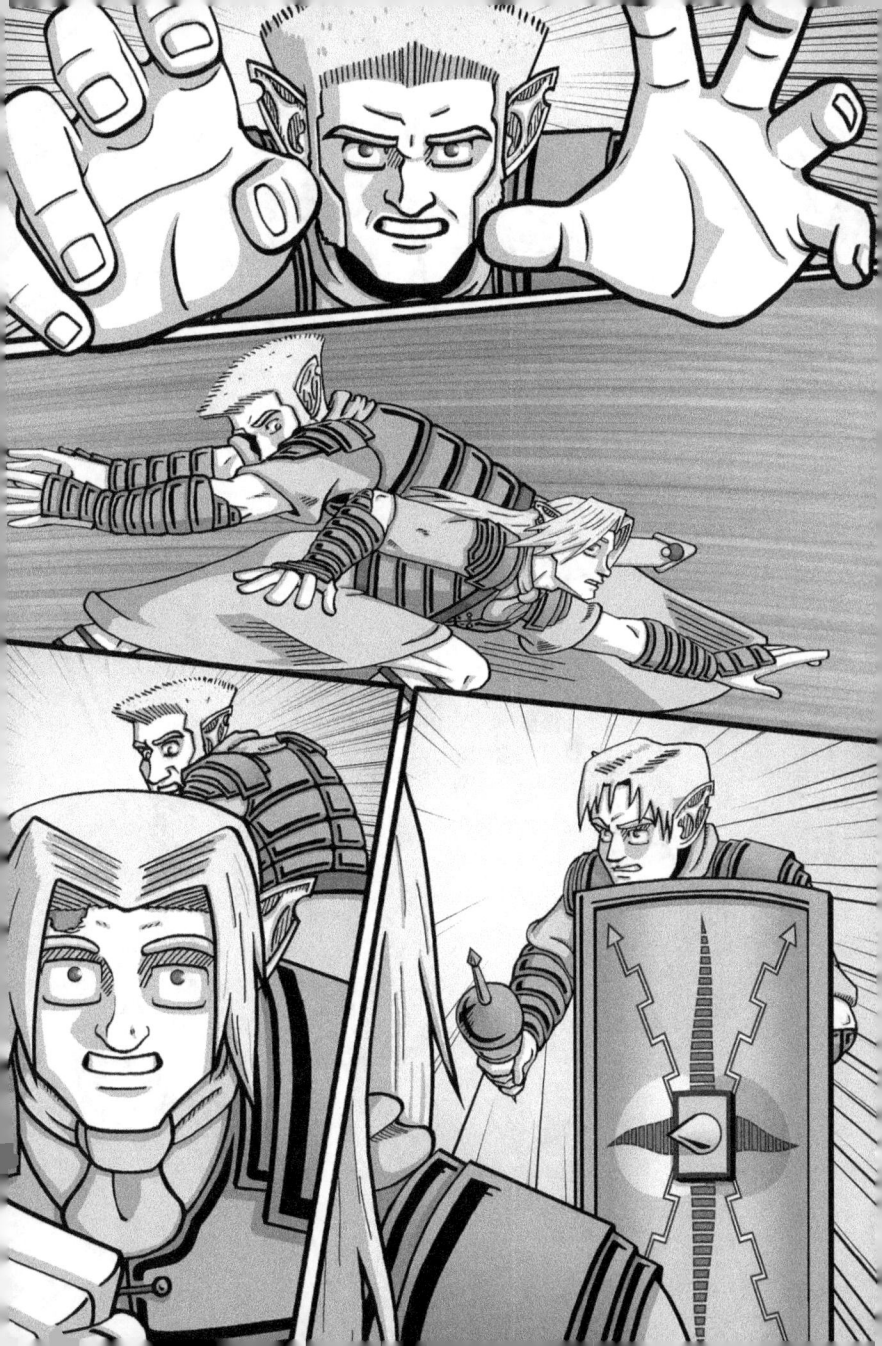

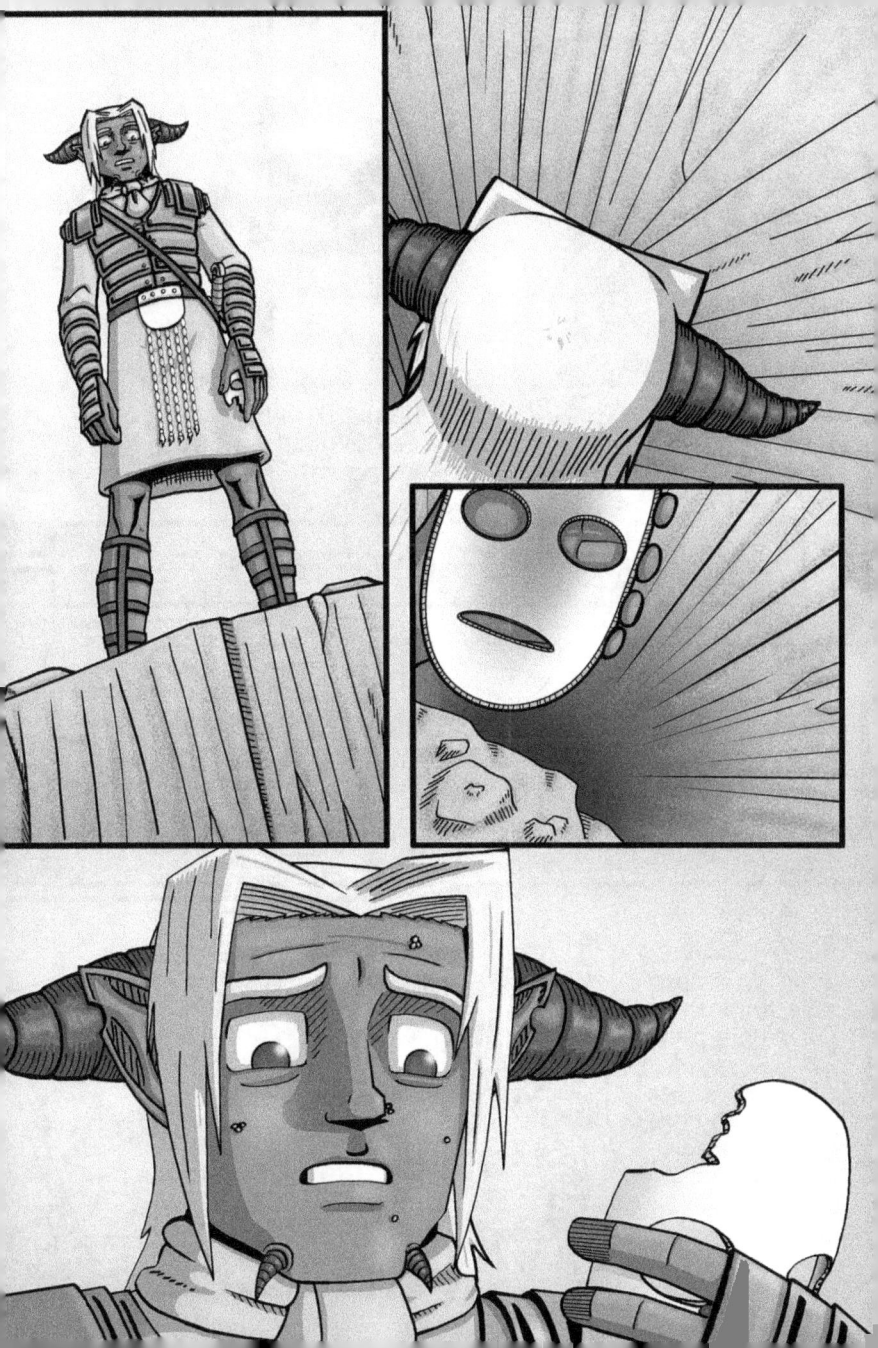

DON'T BE STUPID, CRISPUS..

YOU'RE NOT AT THE END OF THE ROAD YET.

THERE ARE OTHER OPTIONS

IF I GET BETTER AT HUNTING, MAYBE SOME WILD FOLK MIGHT LOOK PAST HOW UGLY I AM...

IF I FIND CIVILISATION, I COULD SELL MY ARMOUR, GET A JOB AND BUY SOME FRIENDS...

CIRCUS FREAK?

MAYBE I COULD FIND SOME BLIND—

HM?

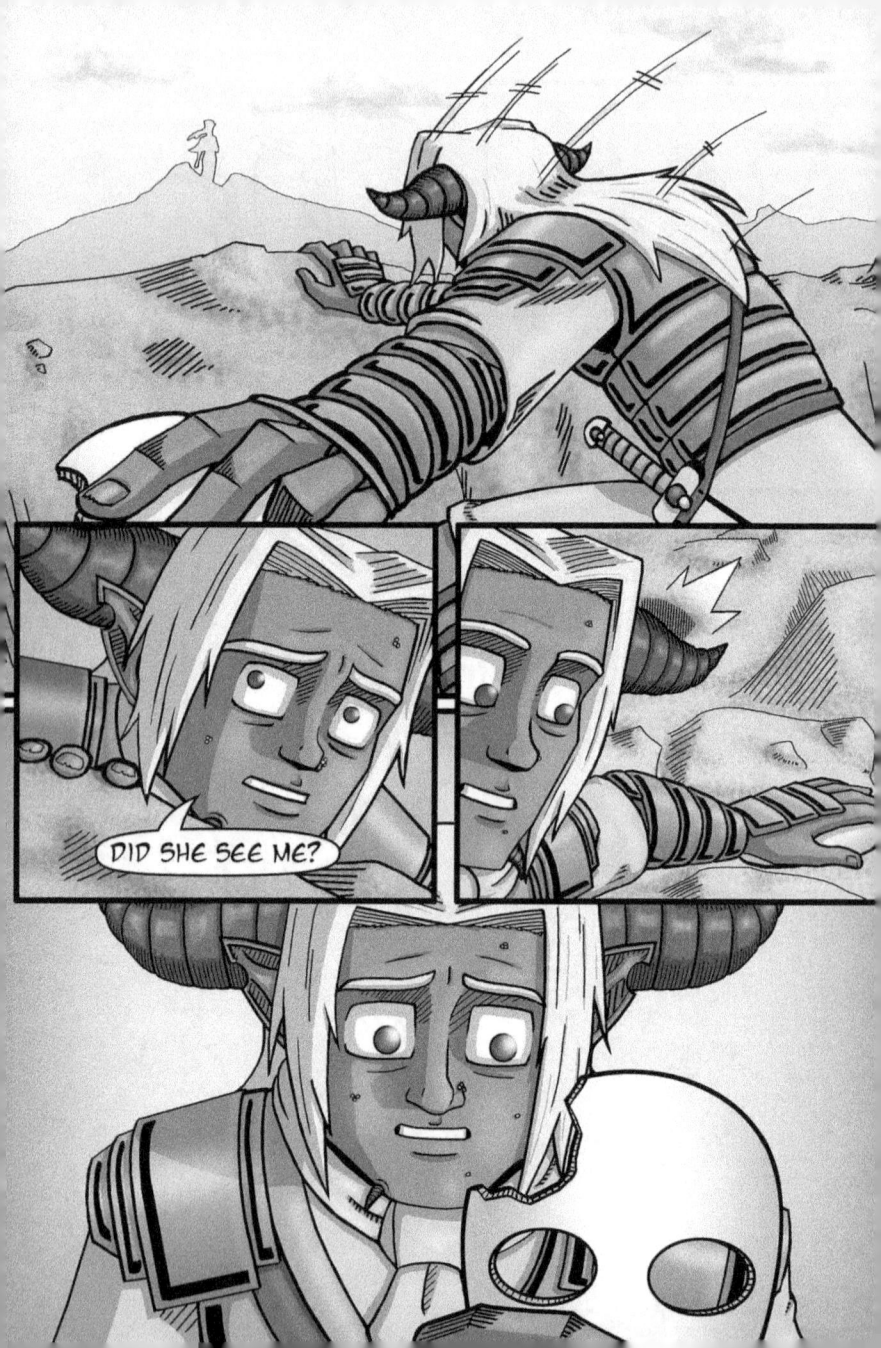

AVE!

YOU LOOK LOST.

I SAID FORGET IT!

HEY!

I HAVE FOOD BACK AT MY CAMP!

...FOOD

VERY WELL.

SHRILLHOUND.
YEP.
I NOTICE YOU FAILED TO MENTION THAT SHRILLHOUND WAS YOUR 'FOOD'.
YA-HUH.
IT MIGHT BE BETTER JUST STARVE...
UH-HUH.

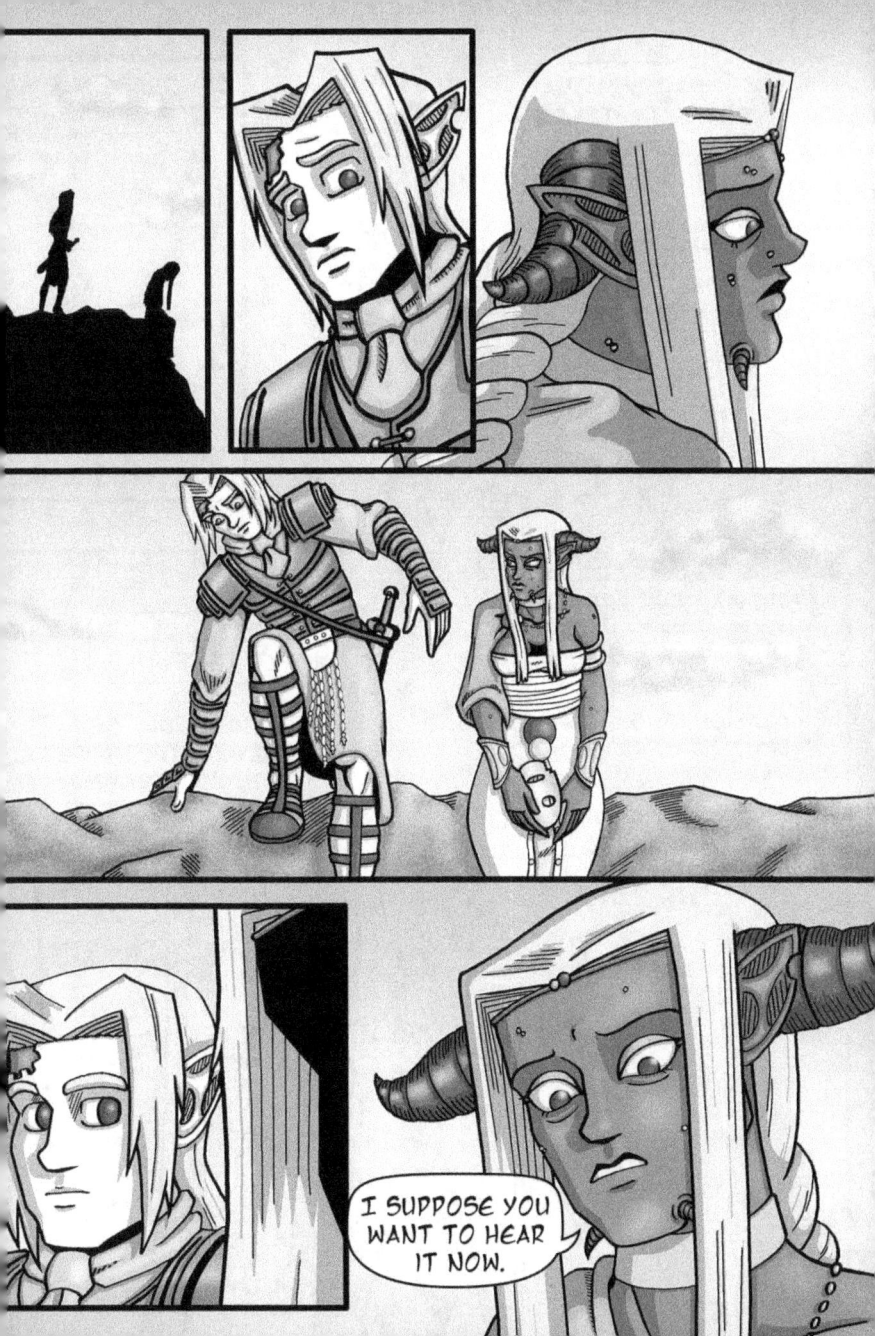

DADDY HAD A PERFECT LITTLE GIRL.
OF COURSE SHE WA
DADDY WAS A SENATO
SHE WAS THE PRETTIEST.
SHE WAS THE MOST GLAMOUROUS.
SHE DATED ALL THE HOTTEST GUYS.
SHE WOULD BE THE GREATEST WIFE IN HYPOCRIUM.

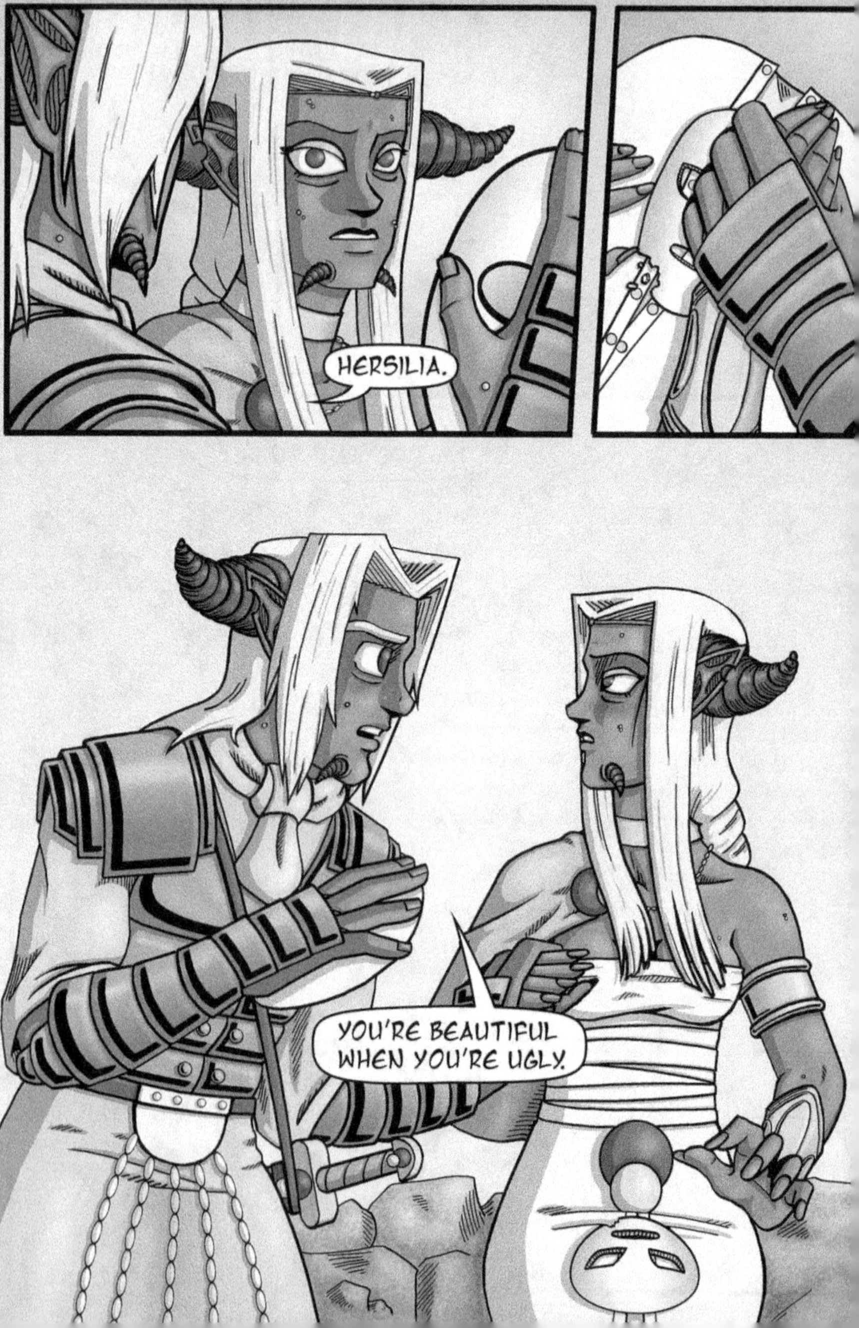
HERSILIA.
YOU'RE BEAUTIFUL WHEN YOU'RE UGLY.

CLANG!

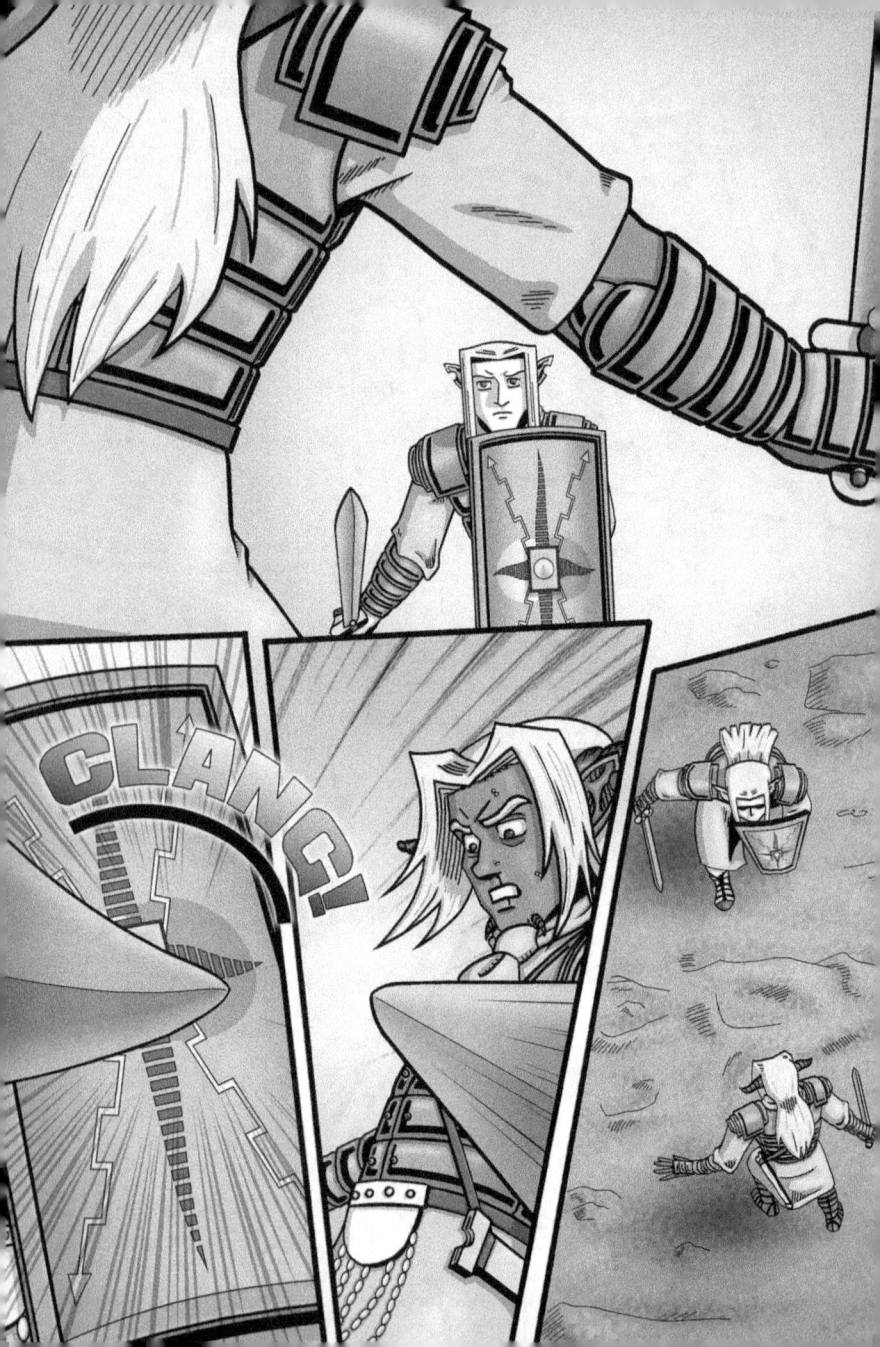

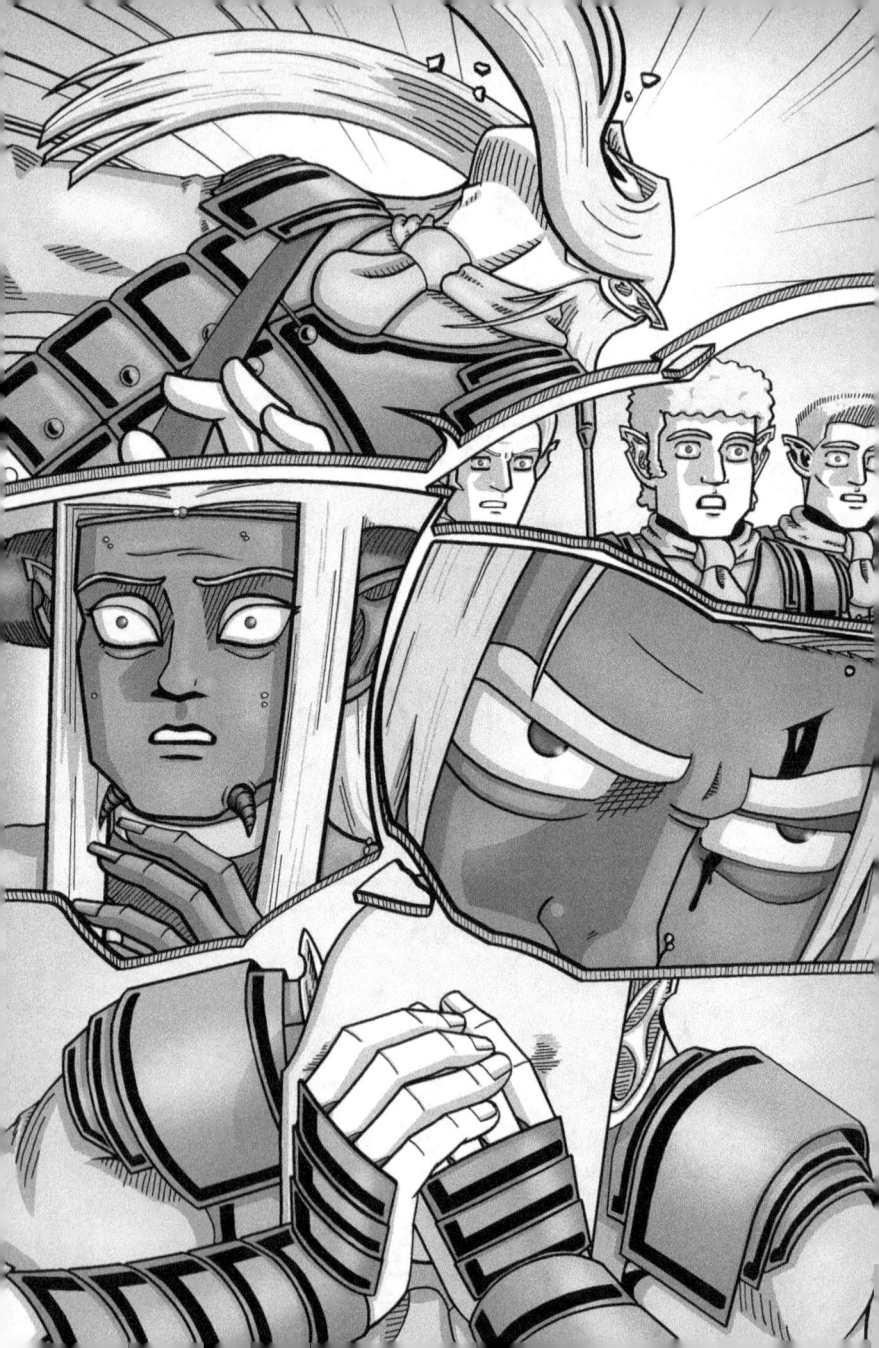

WHAT THE HELLS IS THIS?

DON'T LOOK AT ME!

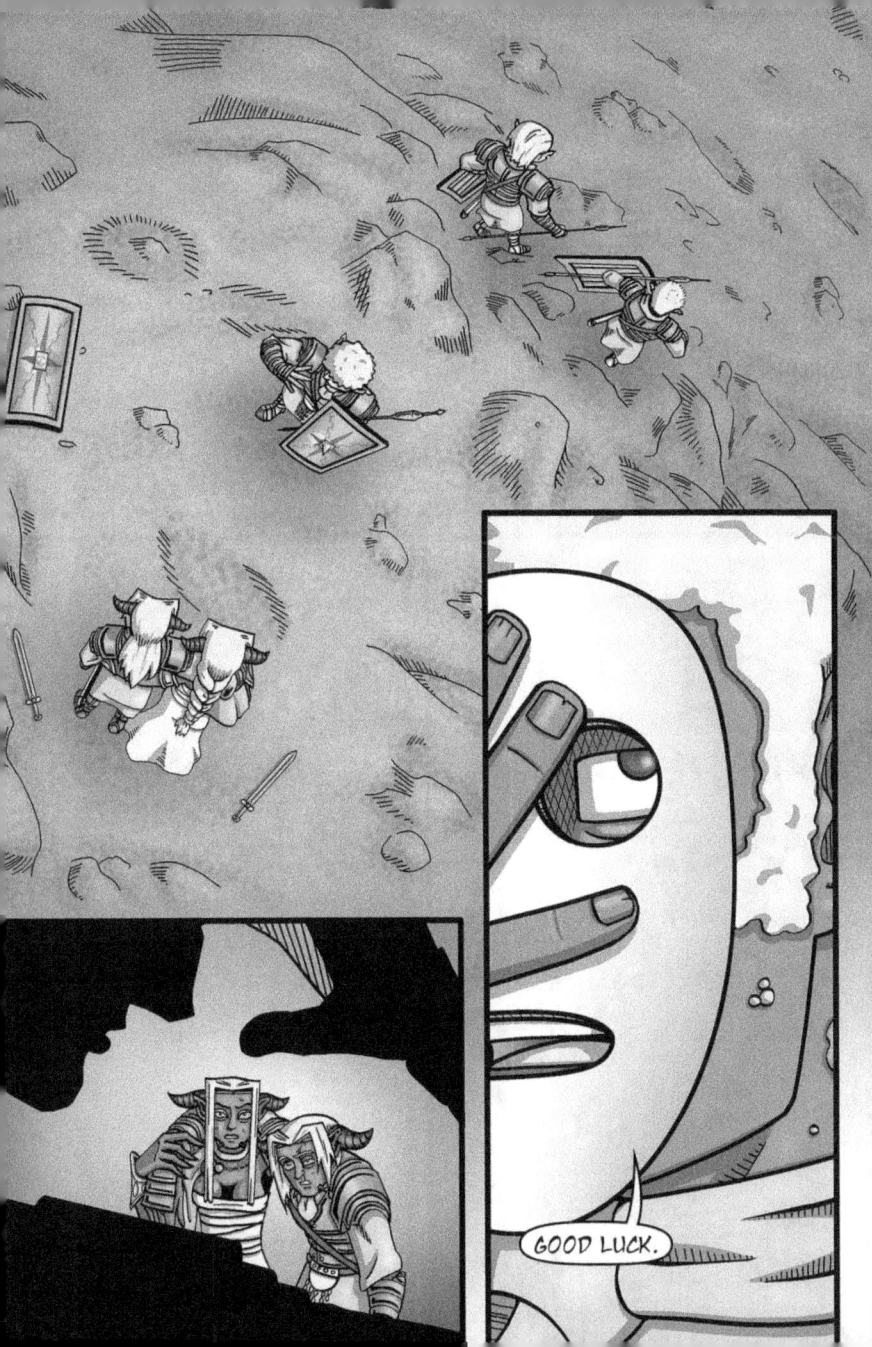

GOOD LUCK.

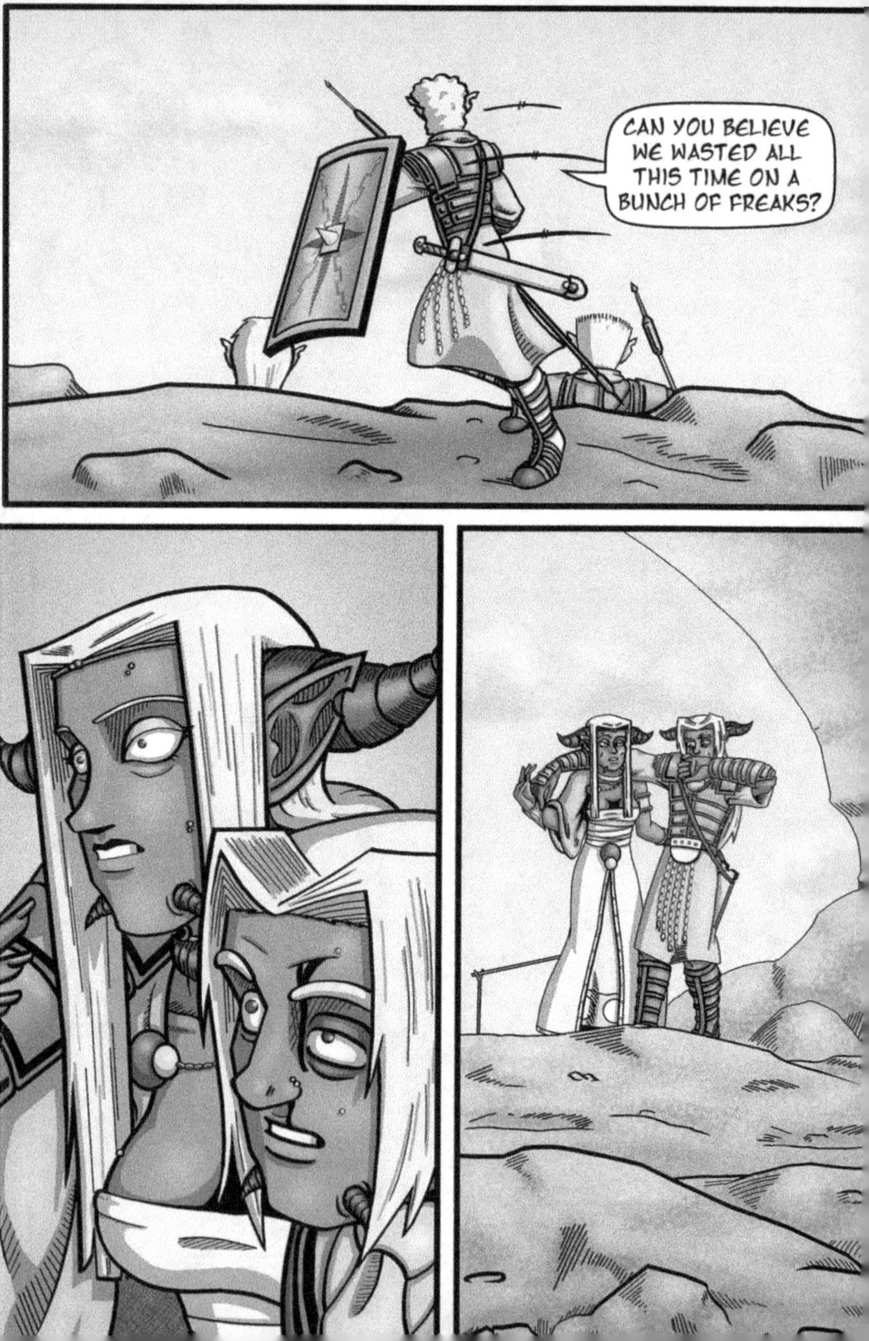

CAN YOU BELIEVE WE WASTED ALL THIS TIME ON A BUNCH OF FREAKS?

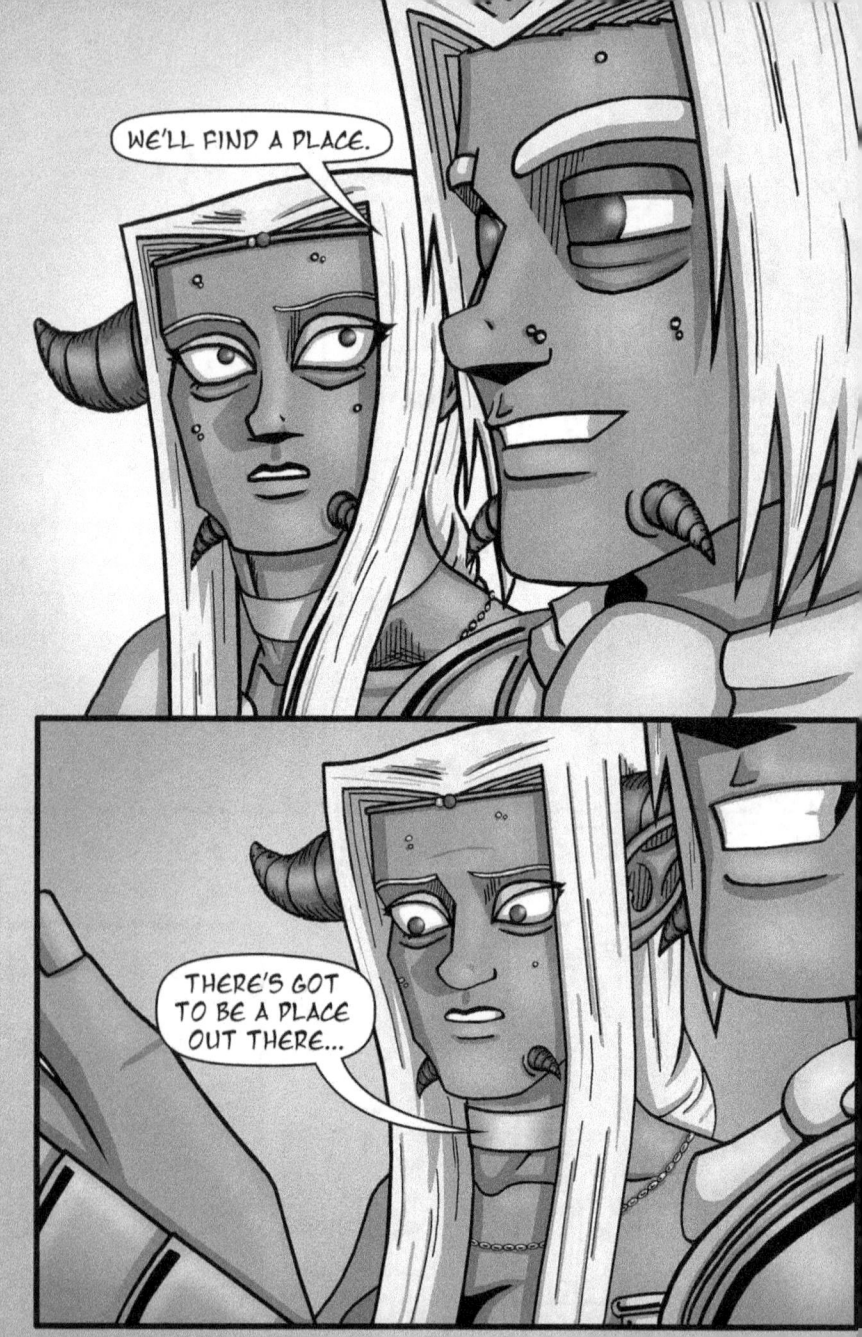

THANKS FOR SUPPORTING MASK!

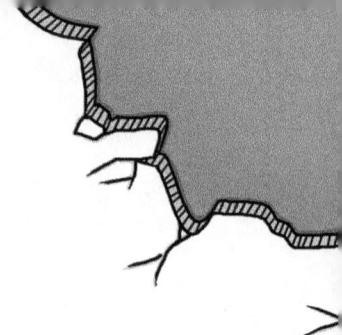